Book Ten

Contributing Authors

Bellwood Public School-Mrs. Amanda Langeveldt & Ms. Jamila Douglas

Mustafa Alsadoon

Liam Brundle

Nicole Bui

Alexander Chimpiringa

London Furnis

Shehzeen Hossain

Maria Kenaan

Siddharth Kesavan,

Elise Logue

Farhaan Pathan

Muaaz Rehan

London Robinson

Jonah Schultheis

Contributing Authors

Bellwood Public School-Mrs. Amanda Langeveldt & Ms. Jamila Douglas

Gavin Sweeting	Violet Goodison
Thashni Theeban	Beckham Lake
Noah Wood	Kyle Mathewson
Aamir Ali Shah	Dylan Mosher
Aaron Ali	Emily Rehberger
Maryam Desai	Robert Zammit-Lawson
Julien Gemmiti	

Contributing Authors

Arklan Community Public School- Bruce Patterson

Sabastian Bellefeuille

Kaia Brake

Avelyn Carruthers

Anna Chapman

Bryant Charron

Nicholas Culhane

Tori Darragh

Kaelan Dullemond

Ryder Gartner

Tye Gillis

Kaydence Guy

Charlotte Henry

Aubree Hunt

Hudson Jardine

Jacob MacIssac

Parker Tait

Ivy Wallace

Owen Causton

Audrey Musker

Contributing Authors

Cobblestone Elementary School-Faye Ferraccioli

Olivia Bingeman

Olivia Birch

Ledger Brown

Gwendolyn Cameron

Hannah Falconer

Adam Gagliardi

Jamie Gray

Nicole Hibbs

Tyson Hockley

Chloe Lanigan

Peyton Lucier

Easton Martin

Brayden Miller

David Milline

Chloe Murray

Cameron Stewart

Madison Straus

Carter Williamson

Ivy Winegarden

Will Yurkiw

Contributing Authors

W.O. Mitchell Elementary - Mrs. Nancy Poirier

Kaiden Bowen

Owen Chen

Reid Flick

Myia Harris

Julia Hazelton

Peyton Holden

Jack Holmes

London Knight

Anna Korchinski

Caleb McGloin

Jeffrey Menard

Chloe Milley

Brooklynn Onofrychuk

Megan Peck

Rena Qian

Christian Ticlea

Sydney Van Dalen

Max Vennor

Ben Walsh

Brett Whiting

Victoria Zolotov

Contributing Authors

Davenport Public School- Miss Beth Buchanan

Ashley Shea

Alan Wall

Sienna Pratt

Rayya McLeod

Holden Gibbons

Ruben Quiring

Nathan Killins

Contributing Authors

Central Public School- Melissa Marteleira

Aries Bray

Mohamad

Brandon Price

Emma Price

Emilia Ambrose

Zoe Martin

Erika Cox-Skinner

Semiah Martin

Kezia Hammond

Connor Goodale

Taeus Peterson-Moore

Ciarra Turkey

Jack Sabatini-Carew

Aya

ACKNOWLEDGMENTS

A very special thank you to all those who help make Write to Give happen. Each year, the program continues to grow and have a bigger impact on Canadian and international students. This would not happen, if it were not for the hard work of the teachers who have helped implement this program.

Thank you to our teachers, Mrs. Langeveldt, Jamila Douglas, Mr. Patterson, Mrs. Ferraccioli, Mrs. Poirier, Miss Beth Buchanan, Mrs. Marteleira!

Thank you to my team of editors, designers and family who have helped with W2G 2017.

Thank you,   Amy McLaren

x

The Acacia Tree
A Lesson in Kindness

Copyright © 2017

xi

In the heart of Kenya, among vast, endless grasslands, where the sun casts its hazy glow, animals, so diverse in nature, are free to roam across a wide, open terrain.

Within that country, grew a very special Acacia tree. This tree was known by every creature as 'Hisani', meaning 'Kindness' in Swahili.

This tree was often celebrated for its ability to care for the many creatures that sought shelter, food and protection there.

From the largest of animals to the smallest of insects, 'Hisani' graciously provided.

Giraffes frequently ate the leaves that grew in the upper canopy of the tree, by stretching their long necks.

Colourful birds made their homes in the shelter of the branches. Hisani also provided protection from the hot Savannah sun for other animals, such as lions.

They would often be found taking their afternoon naps in the shade of the tree, while ants made their home within the thorns on the trunk.

Hisani was true to its name; however, would its occupants respect everything it had to offer, and show the same kindness in return?

Hisani's abilities to provide for all of the Kenyan animals quickly spread across the Savannah. The giraffes told the elephants about the sweet tasting leaves. The birds told the monkeys about the comfortable branches, perfect for swinging and sleeping on. The lions told the leopards and cheetahs about the nice, cool shade the tree had.

Hisani started to feel heavy and crowded from all of the animals. The sweet leaves turned brown and began to fall on the ground. The branches started to crack and break from all the weight of the birds and monkeys. The nests of the birds' crashed down to the ground and broke into thousands of pieces.

The shade slowly disappeared as the tree lost its beautiful canopy. The elephant's heavy weight began to crack the soil beneath the tree causing the tree's roots to come out of the ground.

The animals started to blame each other for the mess they had created. The giraffes used their long legs to trip the lions and the elephants stomped on the ground, scaring the birds. Seeing the chaos her kindness had caused Hisani didn't know what to do to fix the mess.

The wise elephant was the first to notice the dying leaves falling off the trees. The giraffes and monkeys tried to stick the leaves back on, but the leaves would not stick. The elephants and lions desperately tried to stick the roots back in the ground but the roots poked back up.

Within a few weeks, the Hisani tree was dead. The community of animals was devastated, The Acacia tree was kind and giving to the end, but was it the end?

Under the full African moon, the animals hatched an idea. With tools, saws, nails and sweat, the animals planned and cut up the huge old tree.

After many days of hard work, they constructed a huge tree house with shade and peace for the big animals, shelves and places for birds and nests and a big stump for the insects to live in. There were even bars and swings for the monkeys.

Even though Hisani was gone, the kindness the animals had learned from Hisani lived on. The animals took the seeds of Hisani and spread them throughout the terrain.

The next spring, hundreds of Hisani's children sprouted.

The animals returned the kindness by watering and nurturing Hisani's baby trees. The grateful animals also taught the young trees, the kindness shown by their Mother Tree. The Acacia tree named Hisani.

Ten years had passed, the Acacia trees continued to grow bigger and stronger each day. The young Acacia trees and animals soon learned the story of Hisani. The Acacia trees were never taken advantage of again. The young Acacia trees and animals continued spreading the word of kindness.

From then on the animals were taken care of with food, shelter, and shade. The next generation of animals told their offspring the story of Hisani. This became a tradition that never died.

🌐 World Teacher Aid

World Teacher Aid is a Canadian charity committed to improving education throughout the developing world with a focus on IDP settlements (Internally Displaced Persons – communities that have been uprooted from their homes). Our current projects are within Kenya and Ghana.

As a charity we are committed to providing access to education for students within settled IDP Camps. We accomplish this vision through the renovation and/or construction of schools.

Before we begin working with a community, we ensure that they are on board with the goal. A community must be settled and show leadership before we commit to a project. We also look for commitment from the Government, ensuring that if we step in and build the school, that they will help support the ongoing expenses, such as teachers salaries, and more.

AUTOGRAPHS

AUTOGRAPHS

70866007R00020

Made in the USA
Columbia, SC
19 May 2017